JUNIPER JUPITER

LIZZY STEWART

Lincoln
Children's Books

For my friends, who are all super-heroes —L.S.

Brimming with creative inspiration, how-to projects, and useful information to enrich your everyday life, Quarto Knows is a favourite destination for those pursuing their interests and passions. Visit our site and dig deeper with our books into your area of interest: Quarto Creates, Quarto Cooks, Quarto Homes, Quarto Lives, Quarto Drives, Quarto Explores, Quarto Gifts, or Quarto Kids.

Juniper Jupiter © 2018 Quarto Publishing plc. Text and illustrations © 2018 Lizzy Stewart

First Published in 2018 by Lincoln Children's Books, an imprint of The Quarto Group, The Old Brewery, 6 Blundell Street, London N7 9BH, United Kingdom.
T (0)20 7700 6700 F (0)20 7700 8066 www.QuartoKnows.com

ISBN 978-1-78603-023-8

The illustrations were created with pencils and watercolour
Set in Caecilia

Designed by Zoë Tucker
Edited by Jenny Broom
Production by Kate O'Riordan

Manufactured in Dongguan, China TL122017

9 8 7 6 5 4 3 2 1

Juniper Jupiter is a super-hero.
A real one. It's no big deal.

She's super-kind
and super-brave,

she's super-fast
and super-sneaky,

she's super-strong

and she's super-super-smart.

And she can fly. But, like I said,
it's no big deal.

Juniper Jupiter loves being
a superhero, she really does.
Only, sometimes, she wishes
it wasn't such a lonely job.

It gets so boring waiting for the super-secret-mission telephone to ring!

What Juniper Jupiter needs is a side-kick!

She can't believe she
hasn't thought of it before!
Everything would be much
more fun with a side-kick.

Juniper starts scribbling down a checklist of things
her side-kick needs to be – brave, strong, smart...

A side-kick absolutely MUST love ice-cream. That's rule number one!

They should be good at dancing.

And a side-kick should be funny. That's very important too.

Juniper puts up posters all over town –
she wants the best of the best.

She wonders if anyone will
come on audition day.

It turns out a lot
of people want to be a
super-hero's side-kick!

An *awful* lot of people!

Juniper isn't daunted, though!
She has a checklist and a brand-new
pencil, and she's ready to go.

The first is
TOO SCRATCHY.

The second is TOO BIG.

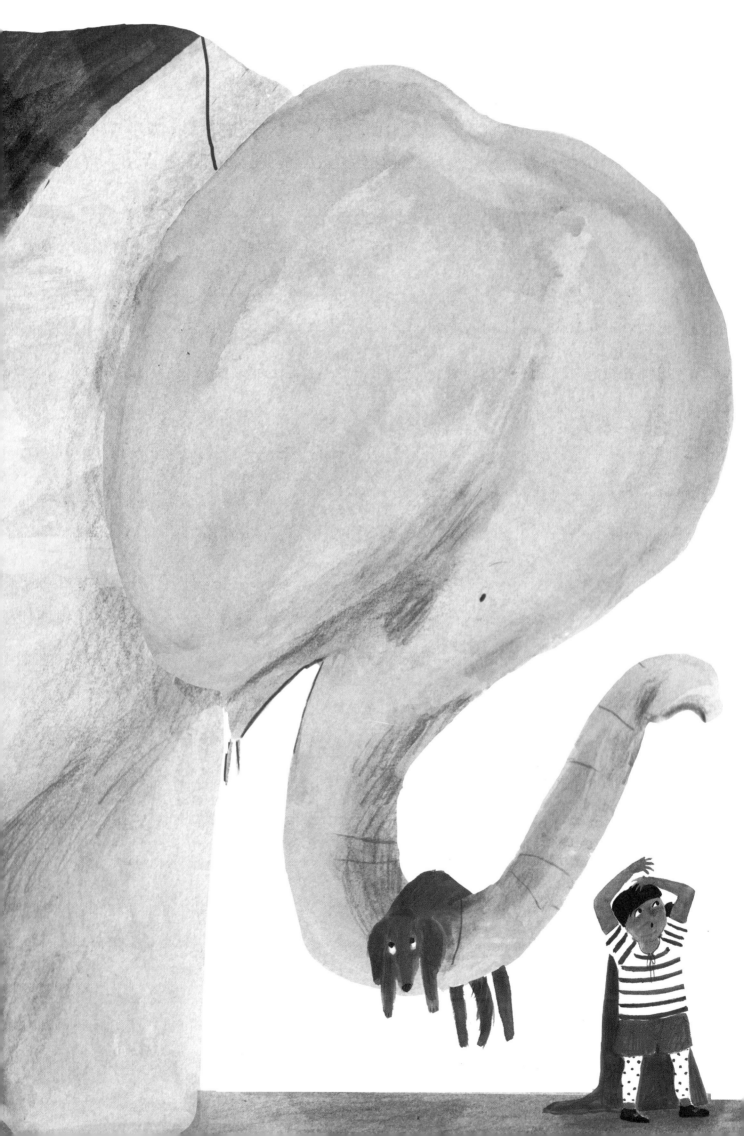

The next are too scared...

Much too prepared...

Too weird...

Too much beard!

"THIS IS USELESS!" sighs Juniper.
"I'm never going to find a good side-kick."

She's all ready for a super-sized sulk when a
shadow appears in the doorway. There's one
more side-kick left to see...

Peanut!

Brave!

Strong!

Funny!

Super!

This one has it all!
Juniper can't believe her luck.

Juniper Jupiter and Peanut
go everywhere together.

Peanut is the perfect side-kick.

She even loves ice cream!

With Peanut at her side,
Juniper Jupiter is twice as SUPER.

But, like I said, it's no big deal.